Trucks line **up!**"

"Trucks with scrapers,

"Trucks in pink.
Trucks in green.
Big Rig—any time you want.

Trucks line up!"

"That should do it.
Here we go."

"Hey," says Pete. "What about me?"

"Ooops. Sorry, Pete.
Red? Blue?
Scraper? Flasher?"

"No,
no, no,
and
**no.**"

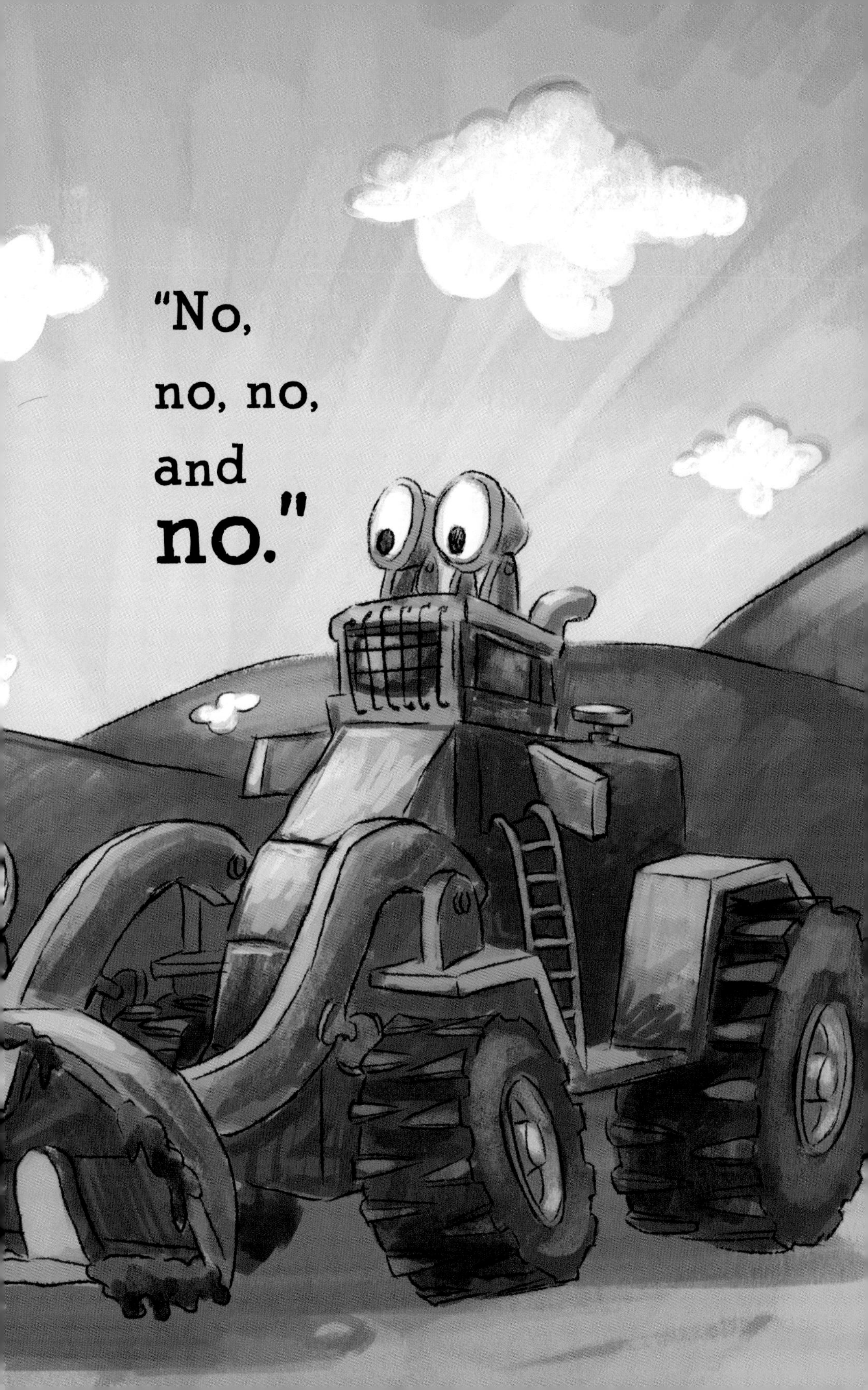

"Um . . .
Orange with scooper,
ladder, muffler,
and a name that starts
with P?"

"Yes!" says Pete.

"Now we are ready.
Every truck.

Ready. Set. Go!"

Trucks go down.

Trucks go
up.

Trucks go round and round and round.

Then Jack honks
his horn and
gives his call:

TRUCKS ...

LINE . . .

. . . UP!

# JON SCIESZKA'S TRUCKTOWN

## TRUCKS LINE UP

### BY JON SCIESZKA

CHARACTERS AND ENVIRONMENTS DEVELOPED BY THE

DAVID SHANNON    LOREN LONG    DAVID GORDON

ILLUSTRATION CREW:

Executive Producer:

INDUSTRIES

Creative Supervisor: Nina Rappaport Brown ○ Drawings by: Dan Root ○ Color by: Antonio Reyna

Art Director: Aviva Shur

## READY-TO-READ

SIMON SPOTLIGHT
NEW YORK    LONDON    TORONTO    SYDNEY

ABDO
Spotlight

## ABDOPUBLISHING.COM

Reinforced library bound edition published in 2016 by Spotlight,
a division of ABDO. PO Box 398166, Minneapolis, Minnesota 55439.
Spotlight produces high-quality reinforced library bound editions for
schools and libraries. Published by agreement with Simon Spotlight.

Printed in the United States of America, North Mankato, Minnesota.
042015        092015

THIS BOOK CONTAINS
RECYCLED MATERIAL

SIMON SPOTLIGHT
An imprint of Simon & Schuster Children's Publishing Division
1230 Avenue of the Americas, New York, NY 10020
First Simon Spotlight paperback edition February 2011
Copyright © 2011 by JRS Worldwide, LLC. TRUCKTOWN AND JON SCIESZKA'S
TRUCKTOWN and design are trademarks of JRS Worldwide, LLC. All rights reserved,
including the right of reproduction in whole or in part in any form. SIMON SPOTLIGHT,
READY-TO-PEAD, and colophon are registered trademarks of Simon & Schuster, Inc.

## LIBRARY OF CONGRESS CATALOGING-IN-PUBLICATION DATA

*This title was previously cataloged with the following information:*

Scieszka, Jon.
  Trucks line up / by Jon Scieszka ; artwork created by the Design Garage: David
Gordon, Loren Long, David Shannon. — 1st Simon Spotlight ed.
  p. cm. — (Ready-to-read) (Jon Scieszka's Trucktown)
Summary: As soon as Jack Truck wakes up he gets the other trucks in line, but
somehow he misses Pete.
[1. Trucks--Fiction.] I. Design Garage. II. Title.
PZ7.S41267Tnt 2011
[E]—dc22

                    2009035952

978-1-61479-398-4 (reinforced library bound edition)

 Spotlight     A Division of ABDO     abdopublishing.com

Jack wakes up.
He gives his call:
"Trucks line up!"

"Blue trucks here.
Red trucks there.